W9-BRV-513

Uncle Andy's CATS

JAMES WARHOLA

G. P. PUTNAM'S SONS

G. P. PUTNAM'S SONS

A division of Penguin Young Readers Group.

Published by The Penguin Group. Penguin Group (USA) Inc., 375 Hudson Street, New York, NY 10014, U.S.A. Penguin Group (Canada), 90 Eglinton Avenue East, Suite 700, Toronto, Ontario M4P 2Y3, Canada (a division of Pearson Penguin Canada Inc.). Penguin Books Ltd, 80 Strand, London WC2R 0RL, England. Penguin Ireland, 25 St. Stephen's Green, Dublin 2, Ireland (a division of Penguin Books Ltd.). Penguin Group (Australia), 250 Camberwell Road, Camberwell, Victoria 3124, Australia (a division of Pearson Australia Group Pty Ltd). Penguin Books India Pvt Ltd, 11 Community Centre, Panchsheel Park, New Delhi - 110 017, India. Penguin Group (NZ), 67 Apollo Drive, Rosedale, North Shore 0632, New Zealand (a division of Pearson New Zealand Ltd). Penguin Books (South Africa) (Pty) Ltd, 24 Sturdee Avenue, Rosebank, Johannesburg 2196, South Africa. Penguin Books Ltd, Registered Offices: 80 Strand, London WC2R 0RL, England.

Copyright © 2009 by James Warhola.

All rights reserved. This book, or parts thereof, may not be reproduced in any form without permission in writing from the publisher, G. P. Putnam's Sons, a division of Penguin Young Readers Group, 345 Hudson Street, New York, NY 10014. G. P. Putnam's Sons, Reg. U.S. Pat. & Tm. Off. The scanning, uploading and distribution of this book via the Internet or via any other means without the permission of the publisher is illegal and punishable by law. Please purchase only authorized electronic editions, and do not participate in or encourage electronic piracy of copyrighted materials. Your support of the author's rights is appreciated. The publisher does not have any control over and does not assume any responsibility for author or third-party websites or their content. Published simultaneously in Canada. Manufactured in China by South China Printing Co. Ltd.

Text set in Bruce Old Style. The art was done in watercolor on Arches paper.

Library of Congress Cataloging-in-Publication Data: Warhola, James. Uncle Andy's cats / James Warhola. p. cm. Summary: Twenty-five cats named Sam have the run of Uncle Andy's (artist Andy Warhol's) New York City townhouse. [1. Cats—Fiction. 2. Warhol, Andy, 1928–1987—Fiction.] I. Title. PZ7.W2345Un 2009 [E]—dc22 2008033699

ISBN 978-0-399-25180-1   10 9 8 7 6 5 4 3 2 1

Dedicated
to my
grandmother—
Julia Warhola

ncle Andy said it all started with a little blue pussycat named Hester. "She was just a kitty when I got her from a fabulous movie star called Gloria."

Little Hester just loved Uncle Andy's house. It was tall and skinny and perfect for dashing up and down stairs and hiding among the antiques.

The only time Hester was still was when she was staring at Grandma Bubba's mynah bird, Echo.

On our visits to Uncle Andy's,
we would look and look but still
couldn't find little Hester.

Little Hester grew and grew **and grew**

Uncle Andy and Bubba thought Hester was lonely. That's when they decided to get Sam.

It was love at first sight.

and   became...

BIG
HESTER.

Uncle Andy enjoyed Sam and Hester's company when he painted late at night in his studio.

And when it was bedtime, the cats' favorite spot was Uncle Andy's wig drawer.

On one visit there were kittens.
Lots and lots of kittens!

Uncle Andy said, "It's so
marvelous! Hester is now a
mommy."

Bubba said, "They all look
like their papa, so let's name
them each Sam."

Holy mackerel!

The little Sams loved their tall, skinny house too.

The only time we ever saw all the
Sams was when Bubba called them for
their favorite meal, oatmeal and liver.

Uncle Andy said that the Sams
liked us best when we were sleeping,
and I think Uncle Andy did too.

We always loved snooping around at Uncle Andy's and one day we got another surprise—Hester and Sam were a mommy and daddy again.

Holy macaroni!

The kittens all looked just like their daddy, so
they were also named Sam and that made for a
whole lot of Sams!

Uncle Andy was sometimes
interrupted when a herd of Sams
would stampede through his studio.
   And the neighbors were interrupted
when the Sams would sneak up to
the roof.

The Sams loved to rumble amongst my uncle's soup boxes.

At the end of a long day, they found that sleeping in Uncle Andy's room was very comfortable.

Now Bubba and Echo had a little bit
too much company. "Andy, there are just
too many Sams!" Bubba told him.
But Uncle Andy didn't know what to do.

We brought three Sams home with us, but that didn't work out too well when they wouldn't come down from the roof.

Holy cat!

Finally, Uncle Andy had a plan.

Uncle Andy and Bubba drew and painted the most marvelous portraits of Hester and the Sams. After many days of working, the art was finally ready to be sent to the printer.

Uncle Andy and Bubba each created a
fabulous book. Uncle Andy's was called
25 Cats Name Sam and One Blue Pussy.
And Bubba named hers *Holy Cats*.

The books were a huge hit and the Sams
became famous overnight. Everybody
wanted a Sam. They came from uptown
and downtown to get a Sam.

In no time at all, things were just about back to normal, and that made Uncle Andy and Bubba very, very pleased.

Holy moley!

As it turned out, Hester and Sam were just the
right amount of cats for their tall, skinny house.